My Cat's Weird

Lydia Monks

My cat's not like other cats.

He's weird!

He doesn't
walk
like other
cats.

He doesn't
sit
like other
cats.

He doesn't **wash** like other cats.

He doesn't **eat** like other cats.

He
doesn't
do
the
things
other
cats
do.

When I pass him in the street, I pretend not to know him.

My friends
laugh at him.
Their pets are
normal.

I wish
mine was!

what's he up to now?

I'm going to keep an eye on him.

What's he doing in a
hardware shop?

Cats don't normally
do DIY!

What's
he doing
with
all
that
rubbish?

**I'm
going
to
tiptoe
after
him.**

BANG!

The shed door **bursts** open.
My cat is flying an aeroplane!

How weird is that?

He grabs my arm and swings me up beside him.
And we're off!
Up, up and away!

Over the house,

over the town, and far, far, far away!

Where are we going?

Where is my cat taking me?

I see
giraffes,
zebras
and
elephants.

With a . . .

bump, **bump,** **bump,**

we land

My cat's cousins have come to meet us!

We sit under a tree,
and have tea and cake.

All too soon, it's time to say goodbye.

I wave to them as they get smaller and smaller!

We loop the loop over the ocean and under the clouds, until I see my shed in the distance.

Next time I see my friends,

I feel so proud!

My cat's not like other cats.
He's weird . . .